THE HAMSTER
BALLET COMPANY

THE HAMSTER BALLET COMPANY

JANIS MITCHELL

Commentaries by Stanley Baron

With 31 color plates

THAMES AND HUDSON

© 1986 Thames and Hudson Ltd, London

First published in the United States in 1986 by
Thames and Hudson Inc., 500 Fifth Avenue,
New York, New York 10110

Library of Congress Catalog Card Number 85-52135

Printed and bound in Hong Kong

The Hamster Ballet Company owes everything to its founder, that extraordinary entrepreneur Igor Gregorevich Hamster. It was the idealism, vision and bull-headed tenacity of this colourful Russian émigré which brought together so many gifted artists – brilliant dancers, choreographers, composers and scenic designers – and made the Company famous throughout the world. A familiar figure, sitting at rehearsals or at daily class, watching or ogling his young company through his famous monocle, he had a particular knack for discovering new talent and was known to nurture his 'baby' ballerinas most carefully.

THE SLEEPING BEAUTY

The Sleeping Beauty was the HBC's first big success. This was largely due to the magnificent sets by Olga Belinsky, and the enchanting performance of Marya Karchova as Princess Aurora. In this picture we see the climactic moment in Act II when Prince Charming, led to King Florestan's palace by the Lilac Fairy, kisses the sleeping princess and awakens her back to life.

Although the original fairy tale, *La Belle au Bois Dormant*, was written by Perrault in the seventeenth century, Belinsky chose to place her settings and costumes in the fourteenth.

THE SLEEPING BEAUTY

One of the great attractions of the HBC's production was the casting of André Balakov in the role of the Bluebird; his elevation was unbelievable.

In the illustrations are three of the charming divertissements in the Wedding Scene, which is the end of the ballet. First the *pas de deux* of the Blue Bird and the Enchanted Princess, full of bravura, athletic dancing. Next, the White Cat and Puss in Boots engaging in a provocative feline courtship. Finally the tale of Red Riding Hood and the Wolf, the latter danced with suave menace by Rudi Cadenza, one of the most admired character dancers in the company.

THE SLEEPING BEAUTY

After the various divertissements performed to entertain the Court (and audience), Princess Aurora and Prince Charming themselves undertake a seductive *pas de deux*.

Marya Karchova, a specialist in the Tchaikovsky ballets, is at her most expressive and lyrical in this role, and is expertly partnered by Ivan Belov.

PETROUCHKA

The HBC production of *Petrouchka* reproduces faithfully the original choreography of Michel Fokine and the sets designed by Alexandre Benois. André Balakov gives a most touching interpretation of the melancholy clown hopelessly in love, but the three principals took quite a time to perfect their puppet-like movements. Working the front paws while dancing with precision is no easy task.

In Scene 3, Petrouchka bursts into the Moor's cell and finds his beloved Ballerina sitting on the Moor's lap. The Ballerina, beautifully danced by one of Igor Gregorevich's 'baby' discoveries, Lisa Malarinsky, professes complete innocence, but Petrouchka is beaten in a fight by the arrogant and all-conquering Moor.

PETROUCHKA

In Scene 4 the crowd attending the Fair witness the Moor killing Petrouchka with his scimitar and rushing away with the Ballerina. A policeman arrives on the scene but the Showman is able to demonstrate to him that Petrouchka is nothing but a stuffed doll.

LA FILLE MAL GARDÉE

La Fille Mal Gardée, first performed by human dancers in 1786, offers an old-fashioned and light-hearted tale which is nothing more than an excuse for some delightful dancing and picturesque effects.

Some of the costumes, such as those of the rooster and chicks in the farmyard scene of Act I, are rather complicated and not altogether comfortable for young hamsters to wear; but Ivan Belov and Daniela Nelitskaya, as Colas and Lise, bring a youthful exuberance and ease to their performances in these roles.

LA FILLE MAL GARDÉE

The Widow Simone, who is so unsuccessful at watching over her daughter Lise, is traditionally performed by a male dancer. Rudi Cadenza attacks the part with great humour and gusto, especially when performing the clog dance.

The part of Alain, the simple-minded suitor for Lise's hand, is less rewarding, but at least in the storm at the climax of Act I, Scene 2, he is spectacularly carried up into the air with his striking red umbrella.

LES SYLPHIDES

This charming invention of Michel Fokine's to various orchestrated piano pieces by Chopin provides an admirable means of showing off the Company's abilities. The *corps de ballet*, all in delicate white costumes, and the soloists perform a number of variations which create a rather wistful, melancholy mood but have no narrative. Ivan Belov is one of the hamster *premiers danseurs* who has been most effective in the man's *pas seul* executed to a Mazurka, and in the Waltz *pas de deux* he provides strong support for Daniela Nelitskaya at her most ethereal.

SWAN LAKE

One of the most popular of all ballets, Tchaikovsky's *Swan Lake*, with Petipa's romantic and demanding choreography, is naturally a staple in the HBC's repertory. It shows off the *corps de ballet* to advantage, and provides brilliant opportunities for Marya Karchova as both Odette and Odile, the White Swan and the Black. Like all the great and famous ballerinas who have mastered these parts, Karchova makes one believe from time to time that she is really a bird and not a hamster.

The scene in the picture is Act II, the lake-side, and shows Odette and Prince Siegfried in the famous *adagio*, as they fall in love at their first meeting.

SWAN LAKE

In Act III, the palace ballroom, Rothbart the enchanter passes off his daughter Odile as Odette. Siegfried is easily deceived and dances as happily with the substitute swan as with the real one. Oblivious to Rothbart's evil designs, he vows that he will make the Black Swan his princess, while Odette, the victim of Rothbart's spell, flutters desperately at the window.

SWAN LAKE

In the last act, the miserably unhappy Siegfried rushes back to
the lake-side in order to explain to Odette how Rothbart tricked
him. He declares his eternal love for her again, but it is too late.
She can no longer escape from the spell which has made her a
swan. Death is the only release. Rothbart appears in the form of
an owl, and gloats over his victory. But the lovers frustrate him,
in true ballet fashion, by choosing to die in the lake.

COPPÉLIA

The background is Galicia, the setting of Act II is the workshop of Dr Coppelius, a toy maker whose various clockwork inventions can be seen in the background. Young Frantz has been given a sleeping draught by the Doctor, and his would-be fiancée, Swanilda, is pretending to be the doll Coppélia come to life.

The combination of Delibes' tuneful score and Saint-Léon's witty choreography has assured *Coppélia* a place in the HBC's repertory. Melanie da Lucca gives a pert and endearing performance in the starring role, managing the doll movements with humorous skill.

GISELLE

This Romantic story of the peasant girl and the disguised prince depends on a prima ballerina of unusual gifts, since she is called on not only to perform complicated choreography, including many *pas seuls*, but also to mime convincingly a young girl's love, joy, dismay and despair.

Igor Gregorevich found the perfect interpreter for this part in his own beloved Olga Rospovna. The leading critics hailed her as a worthy successor to Pavlova, though it is hard to believe that many of them could have seen the great Anna in her heyday.

In Act I Giselle dances an affecting *pas de deux* with Prince Albrecht (acting the part of a farmhand, Loys) while the jealous gamekeeper Hilarion looks on in rage, and Giselle's mother Berthe issues dire warnings that Giselle will dance herself to death and turn into a Wili – one of those young maidens who die before their marriages and cannot rest in their graves.

GISELLE

In Act II, Albrecht grieves at Giselle's grave, but unexpectedly she appears to him, now she has become one of the Wilis who sprout wings and dance by night. The Queen of the Wilis, Myrtha, has directed the unwilling Giselle to lure Albrecht to his death. Rospovna puts every bit of feeling at her disposal into this dramatic episode. As Albrecht, never the most rewarding of male roles, Ivan Belov is both impassioned and stalwart.

LE SPECTRE DE LA ROSE

This one-act ballet by Fokine, set to Weber's *Invitation to the Waltz*, was revived by the HBC only to show off the talents of Knut Henriksen and Annabella Detroit. The slim tale of a young girl who returns from a party, falls asleep as a rose slips out of her hand, and dreams of a grown-up rose in the shape of a handsome young man was established once and for all at its premiere in 1911 by the startling performances of Nijinsky and Karsavina. Igor Gregorevich ruled that his hamsters should in no way seek to imitate that legendary pair, but to establish through their youth alone an atmosphere of fanciful ecstasy. Once they reach maturity, *Le Spectre* will vanish from the repertory.

LA SYLPHIDE

This 1832 Romantic ballet, devised by Filippo Taglioni for his brilliant daughter Marie, with languorous music by Jean Schneitzhoeffer, is refreshingly old-fashioned in our present age of muscular choreography. The HBC's production is a model of traditional amplitude: a huge cast, elaborate costumes, massive scenery.

Act I begins with James Reuben asleep and dreaming of a winged creature, La Sylphide. It is the eve of his wedding to Effie, but he falls in love with this otherworldly charmer. Is she real or imaginary? Diana Forrester, one of several Australians in the company, brings her unusual technical skill to the part, and James is movingly danced and mimed by that nimble French hamster, Hubert d'Albert.

LA SYLPHIDE

Act II is a night scene in a Scottish forest and begins with a gathering of witches. They vanish, as witches do, at dawn, and a moment later James appears in search of his Sylphide. They meet, they dance, they are parted, they find each other again; but of course the outcome is tragic and La Sylphide dies in the arms of her 'sisters'.

THE RITE OF SPRING

The HBC decided to give the first performance of their version of Stravinsky's *Rite of Spring* during their barnstorming tour of the United States. The opening night in Peoria, Ill., was virtually a repeat of the original premiere in Paris in 1913, the final curtain falling to a chorus of boos and catcalls from the audience. Eventually, however, this adaptation of Nijinsky's choreography has settled down as a staple item in the repertory, and the dynamic performance of Natasha Nightfall as the Chosen Maiden makes a rousing, pulsating climax.

ROMEO AND JULIET

When it occurred to Igor Gregorevich to mount this ballet, he decided to do something entirely original. No Prokofieff music, not even Tchaikovsky! He invited the *avant-garde* American composer Hal Sentry to provide a dance score using a 'cello, a celesta, a banjo, and gongs. Though the music is not particularly suited to the tragic story, this results in an interesting tension, which seems to have satisfied large audiences. Trevor Hambleton's choreography combines classical movements with elements from Martha Graham and Merce Cunningham, but he follows the plot closely, as in this scene showing the clash of Capulets and Montagues in the market square of Verona.

ROMEO AND JULIET

The rapturous scene in Juliet's bedroom. Melanie da Lucca and
Homer Whitestock, Igor Gregorevich's most recent American
discovery, perform a fluid, waltz-like *pas de deux* to a banjo solo.

L'APRÈS-MIDI D'UN FAUNE

Some thought that the idea of a hamster dressing up to look like a faun, and executing an archaic, somewhat erotic dance, was faintly ludicrous. But Knut Henriksen's performance put all doubts at rest. Virtually a child when he first undertook the role, Knut seemed to embody the spirit of Mallarmé's impressionistic poem, and of course the Debussy score never fails to underline the implications of Nijinsky's sensual choreography.

CINDERELLA

This evergreen fairy-tale has had many incarnations on the ballet stage. The HBC has mounted it in traditional style, using the sprightly Prokofieff music and the free-flowing choreography of Sir Frederick Ashton.

In Act I, the Ugly Sisters (played by Rudi Cadenza and Hubert d'Albert) preen themselves in anticipation of the Prince's ball. Poor Cinderella, left behind to tend the hearth after her family leave, dances alone, pretending that her broom is the Prince. This is a charming part for Olga Rospovna, but it suits the talents of Diana Forrester almost as well.

CINDERELLA

Act II is the splendid ballroom scene. Cinderella, who has after all appeared at the ball thanks to the fairy godmother, makes a strong impression on Prince Charming, and participates in a *pas de deux* with him while the Fairies of the Four Seasons hover near by.

THE FIREBIRD

This Stravinsky-Fokine classic, first produced in 1910, was successfully revived by Igor Gregorevich as a vehicle for Natasha Nightfall. She and André Balakov are particularly effective in Scene I where Ivan Tsarevich watches the Firebird plucking a golden apple from an enchanted tree. At first he tries to capture her, but he spares her and in return she gives him a feather with magic properties from her breast.

THE NUTCRACKER

What would Christmas be without *The Nutcracker*? How would children ever be introduced to the world of ballet otherwise?

The HBC produces the old ballet as an opulent romp, full of unexpected scenic effects created by Olga Belinsky, and giving an opportunity to young hamster aspirants to set their toes upon the stage for the first time.

Act I begins with the Christmas party scene in Dr Stahlbaum's house. In the midst of the fun and games, the mysterious Drosselmeyer appears, along with his young nephew. He gives Marie, the young daughter of the house, a curious little wooden soldier which is in fact a Nutcracker.

THE NUTCRACKER

In Act I, Scene 2, the magic begins. The Nutcracker becomes as large as Marie, and through Drosselmeyer's ministrations, the Christmas tree grows bigger and bigger until its white branches dominate the back of the stage. The *corps de ballet* are meant to represent snowflakes.

THE NUTCRACKER

The divertissements in Act II are danced to some of
Tchaikovsky's most familiar music. In the Kingdom of Sweets,
Marie and Drosselmeyer's nephew are entertained by the Sugar
Plum Fairy. In the picture are the five Mandarin Teas, the little
Marzipan clowns and finally the Sugar Plum Fairy herself in a
pas de deux with her Cavalier.

LA BOUTIQUE FANTASQUE

Massine's fantastic one-act ballet of a shop and its customers and its mechanical dolls was introduced into the HBC repertory as a tribute to its highly gifted choreographer. Most people react most enthusiastically to the spirited dance of the Cossack soldiers.

A rather unkind critic wrote of this production, 'Though a lot seems to be going on, nothing much happens.'

. . . And finally – after all the preparations, the practice, the rehearsals – the performance is over, followed by the curtain-calls. The company are naturally gratified by the 'Hurrah's, the 'Bravo's, the flowers and the thunder of applause. But Igor Gregorevich, watching with some pride from the wings, is already planning a new work, trying to decide whether petite Veronica Close is ready for a starring role, assessing the potentialities of a new patron, etc., etc.